Fred Rogers PRODUCTIONS

Donkey Hodie™

Donkey's Awesome, Extra Fun, Very Good Day!

Adapted by Patty Michaels
Based on the screenplay "Donkey's Bad Day"
written by Liz Hara

Simon Spotlight
New York   London   Toronto   Sydney   New Delhi

SIMON SPOTLIGHT
An imprint of Simon & Schuster Children's Publishing Division
1230 Avenue of the Americas, New York, New York 10020
This Simon Spotlight edition August 2022
© 2022 The Fred Rogers Company.
Donkey Hodie is produced by Fred Rogers Productions and Spiffy Pictures.
For information about special discounts for bulk purchases, please contact
Simon & Schuster Special Sales at 1-866-506-1949 or business@simonandschuster.com.
Manufactured in the United States of America 0722 LAK
2 4 6 8 10 9 7 5 3 1
ISBN 978-1-6659-1911-1 (pbk)
ISBN 978-1-6659-1912-8 (ebook)

Donkey Hodie woke up one morning to a loud ringing sound. **"Good morning, alarm clock,"** she said. "Thanks for the wake-up call!"

But as she reached over to turn off the alarm clock, it fell off her nightstand and landed . . . right on her foot!

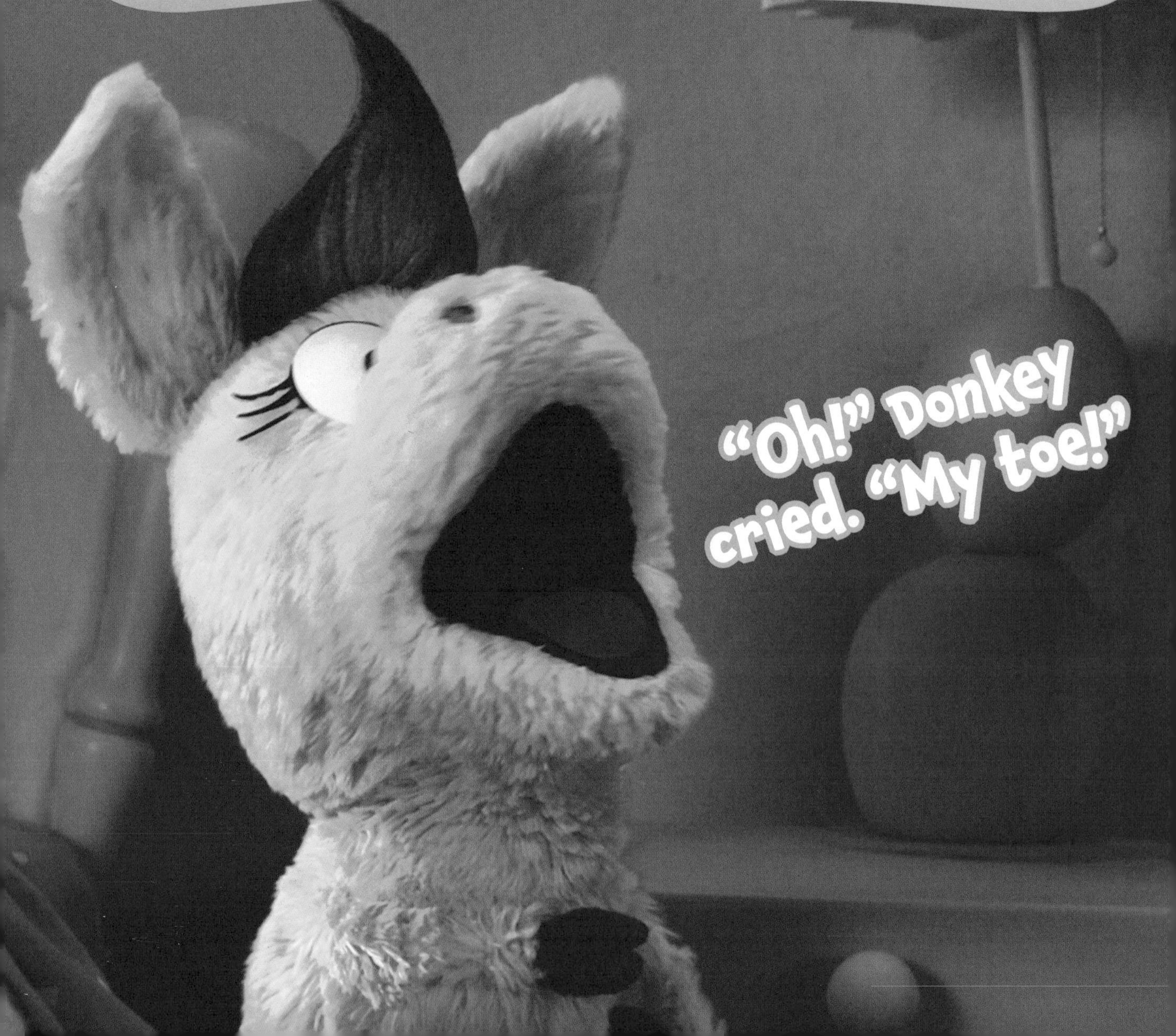

"Oh!" Donkey cried. "My toe!"

Donkey quickly recovered. "No problem!" she said. "Because today is going to be an awesome, extra fun, *very* good day. I am pumped!" But at that moment, Donkey tripped over the alarm clock!

"That's okay," she told herself as she got up. "It's just a bumpy start, that's all. Today is still going to be a great day. I can feel it!"

Just then, Donkey's doorbell rang. It was her best pal, Purple Panda!

"Panda, I have great news," Donkey told him. **"Today is going to be an awesome, extra fun, _very_ good day!"**

"I had a hunch it might be," Panda replied. "So I wore my bow tie. I like to feel fancy!" He gave his bow tie a wiggle.

"Today we're going to have our number one most favorite breakfast!" Donkey told Panda.

"Crunchdoodles!" they cheered.

"And it's special because we're eating Crunchdoodles together," Donkey said.

"Yeah!" Panda agreed. "Crunchdoodles *and* frienddoodles! That's all I need for a great day."

"Good thing I got a brand-new box of Crunchdoodles," Donkey said.

"Where are the bowls?" Panda asked.

As Donkey looked for the bowls, she accidentally knocked over the box of cereal!

"Today is NOT an awesome, extra fun, very good day. Today is officially BAD! Grr!" Donkey grunted and stomped away.

Donkey was feeling very upset. Panda went to go talk to her.
"Hey, Donkey," Panda began slowly. "Are you mad?"
"YES!" Donkey replied. "I'm mad at TODAY! I'm mad and sad and grumpy."

"I'm sorry you're having a bad day," Panda said. "But I think I know what might cheer you up!" He grabbed his ukelele and started to play a song.

But Donkey wasn't feeling much better. Panda tried something else. He put on his clown costume to try and make Donkey laugh. Then he dressed up as a magician and did tricks. But that didn't cheer up Donkey either.

"Maybe we could read a book together," Donkey suggested. She grabbed their favorite book about bugs off the shelf, but then she dropped the book on her foot!

"Ah!" Donkey cried.

"Donkey! Are you okay?" Panda asked worriedly.

"NO! I am not okay!" Donkey shouted. "Today was supposed to be an awesome, extra fun, very good day, but things keep going wrong! Then, when I try to make things better, I make them worse."

"I QUIT today," Donkey continued. **"I, Donkey Hodie, am going back to bed."** Then Donkey went upstairs to her bedroom.

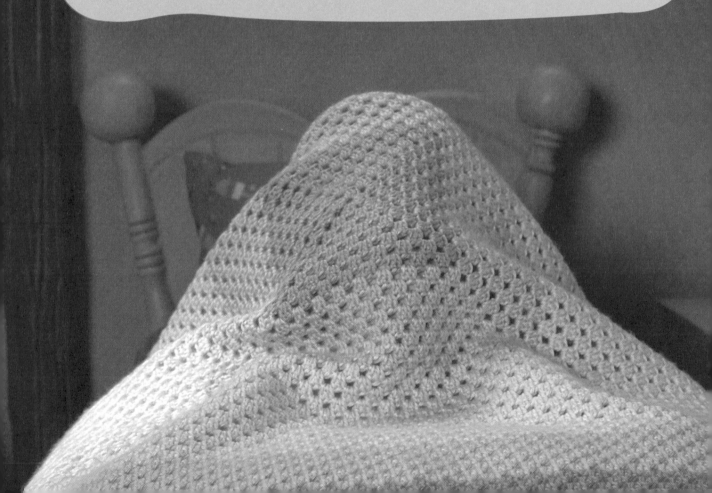

A few minutes later, Panda went to check on her. Donkey was under her blanket. "Hey, buddy," Panda said.

"Panda!" Donkey said. "You're still here? Even though I'm 'un-cheer-up-able'?"

"Of course," Panda replied. "You don't always have to be happy for me to like spending time with you."

"Thanks, Panda," Donkey said. **"You're a true-blue purple pal."**

"I'm always here to help," Panda said.

"Well, I think I just need to be sad right now," Donkey admitted.

"That's okay," Panda said. "I can help with that too. Not to brag or anything, but I have some very soft shoulders. You can lean on them if you want."

Donkey snuggled next to Panda happily.

Suddenly, Panda realized something.

"Donkey!" he said. "Your alarm clock is on the floor! I don't want you to step on this. That would make anyone grumpy!"

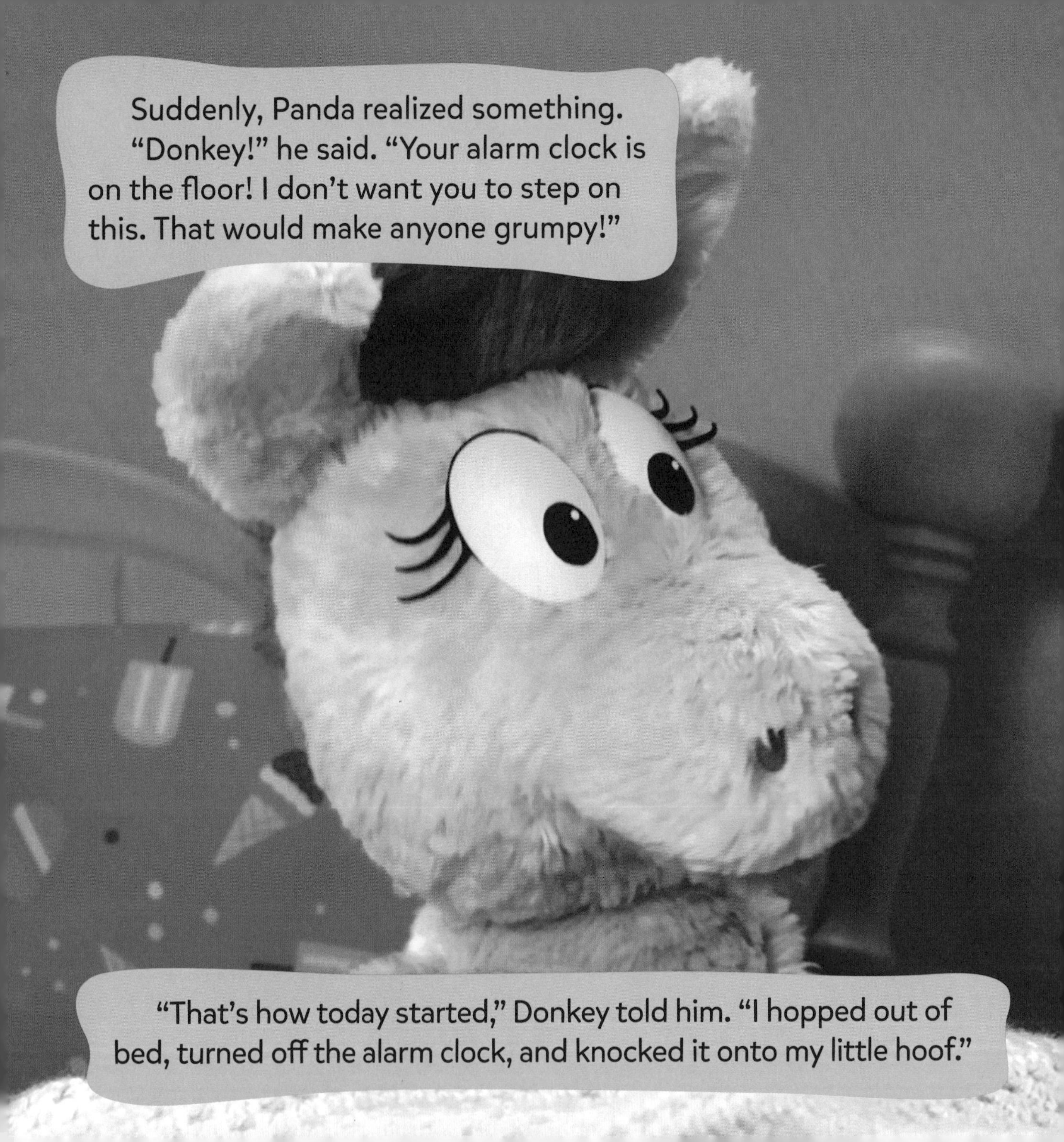

"That's how today started," Donkey told him. "I hopped out of bed, turned off the alarm clock, and knocked it onto my little hoof."

"The left one?" Panda asked. "But that's your favorite hoof!"

"I know," Donkey said. "And I've been kind of grumpy since this morning!"

"That's a long time to be grumpy," Panda told her.

"*Too* long," Donkey agreed. "I'm tired of being grumpy. There's got to be something I can do to cheer myself up. **Think, Donkey Hodie, think!**"

"While you think, I'll hide the clock," Panda told Donkey. "That way you won't see it and remember all the things that went wrong today."

"You're right! Looking at the clock makes me grumpy. . . . Hey, wait!" Donkey had an idea!

Donkey continued. "If looking at the clock makes me grumpy because it reminds me of my *bad* day, what if I looked at some things that remind me of a *happy* day?"

"Donkey Hodie, that's a great idea!" Panda cheered. "Hey, maybe we can put some things in a box!" Panda found an empty box under Donkey's bed.

"We can call it the **Happy Stuff Box**," Donkey suggested. **"Now, I, Donkey Hodie, will cheer myself up!"**

"Let's get started!" Panda said.

Donkey began to look through her drawers. "Hey, Panda, remember this?" she asked, holding up a packet of flower seeds. "The Ungrowdenia flower?"

"Oh yeah!" he said. They both thought back to the day when they had grown the beautiful flower in her garden. "That was a pretty special day!"

"I'm putting this seed packet in the **Happy Stuff Box** for sure!" Donkey said.

"What else?" Panda wondered.

Just then, Donkey found a shovel.

"Oh yeah!" Donkey exclaimed. "We used this shovel the day we helped King Friday build his sand castle!"

"Hey, Donkey, how about this?" Panda asked, holding up a flag.

"Yes!" Donkey exclaimed. "It's the flag from when we tried to climb Mount Really High Up!"

Donkey smiled as she remembered all her good memories. Panda saw how happy she looked and said, "I think the **Happy Stuff Box** is working!"

Then Donkey and Panda sang a happy song together.

It's okay to be mad.
It's okay to feel sad.
It's okay to have days
that are just going bad.
But when you want to cheer yourself up,
just know—you can!

You can change your mood!
Cheer up, cheer up!
Have a new attitude!
Get up, get up!

You can dance, you can sing, you can play!

You can decide
to have an awesome,
extra fun,
very good day!

"There's just one more thing we need to put in the **Happy Stuff Box**," Panda said. "A picture of the two of us! That'll help us remember that a bad day can become a good day. Like today!"

"Today really is an awesome, extra fun, very good day!" Donkey cheered. "I knew it would be. Thank you, Panda!"